Vroom!

HOT CARS

FERRARI
SPIDER

TABLE OF CONTENTS

SIMPLY THE BEST

Luckily, cars don't brag about themselves. If they could, the 2016 Ferrari Spider 488GTB would never shut up. *Car & Driver*, the world's largest car magazine, named it the number one **exotic** sports car for 2016.

If you see it roaring down the highway, you might just hear the engine say "I'm number one! ...I'm number one!" over and over again.

The Ferrari Spider was not originally named after a spider. It got its name from "speeder," which refers to any car with a convertible roof.

5

It takes only 14 seconds for the 488's hardtop to expand or retract, even when the car is moving.

ITALIAN BEAUTY

The Ferrari 488 Spider is a true Italian beauty. It is **sleek** and low to the ground, but gives the impression that it is ready at any moment to simply explode down the road. It has a two-part **retractable** roof that can open up in good weather and close in bad weather.

Italian style. The interior of the 488 is as beautiful as the car's exterior.

You can download Ferrari engine sounds for your cell phone ringtone!

ITALIAN MUSCLE

The Ferrari Spider looks like a beauty, but it also has brawn. And plenty of it! Its V-8 engine delivers 661 horsepower at 8,000 rpm and 560 pound-feet of torque. That's tech-talk to say that it leaves ordinary sports cars in the dust. It accelerates from zero to 60 miles (96.6 kilometers) per hour in only three seconds. The Spider can reach a top speed of 205 miles (330 kilometers) per hour. That's more than two-and-a-half times the top speed limit on highways in Italy (80 miles or 129 kilometers per hour).

The 488 Spider engine is located in the rear of the car.

Enzo Ferrari
1898 –1988

12

Enzo's Story

Henry Ford and Ferdinand Porsche were engineers. Enzo Ferrari began as a racecar driver. Enzo was born in Modena, Italy, on February 18, 1898. At age 10 he witnessed his first car race. From that time, he was determined to become a racing driver.

Enzo competes in a 1922 auto race. He lost, but won a race in 1924.

In 1924, he won his first race. In March 1947 he produced the first car to finally bear the Ferrari family name, the Ferrari 125. He guided the business until his death at age 90 in 1988. His son Piero now runs the business from Ferrari's headquarters in Maranello, Italy.

The Ferrari factory in Maranello conserves energy by using solar cells and features the widespread use of indoor gardens and trees to make a pleasant workplace.

The Ferrari Testa Rossa won many races in the 1950s.

In 1963, the Ford Motor Company tried to buy Ferrari, but the deal fell through at the last moment.

RACING BLOOD

Ferrari has been a racecar force since the 1930s. Throughout the 1960s, Ferrari was the dominant force in sports car racing, winning the 24 Hours of Le Mans 6 years in a row from 1960 to 1965. The 24 Hours of Le Mans is the world's oldest sports car **endurance** race.

Ferrari racecars are transported to race sites in large trailers.

A Ferrari 250 LM that won the 24 Hours of Le Mans on display at Amelia Island, Florida.

"Think as a winner and act as a winner. You'll be quite likely to achieve your goal."
—Enzo Ferrari

Ferrari is also the most successful team in the history of Formula One racing. The "formula" refers to a set of rules, to which all cars must conform. Formula One cars race at speeds of up to 220 miles (360 kilometers) per hour. Ferrari's 2016 Formula One car is the Ferrari SF16-H Formula One Challenger.

Race driver Phil Hill (below) drives for Ferrari at the 1962 German Grand Prix.

Race driver Sebastian Vettel races to first place in a Ferrari at the 2015 Malaysian Grand Prix.

According to the company, Ferrari has won more than 5,000 racing trophies over the decades.

ROAD CAR EXCELLENCE

At first Enzo Ferrari was only interested in building racecars, not road cars. After his factory was bombed during World War II (1939-45), however, his accountants pleaded with him to rebuild the factory to produce road cars. They persuaded him that, by selling cars to the public, he could make money to fund his racing team.

The Ferrari 166 Inter was a hit between 1948 and 1950.

The Ferrari 250 thrilled drivers in 1952.

Today's Ferraris come in a number of colors, but many buyers choose red. Red represents 45 percent of Ferraris sold.

Ferrari perfection. The 1972 Ferrari 365GTS/4 Daytona Spyder now sells as a pre-owned car for between one and two million dollars!

Enzo Ferrari reluctantly agreed with them. He insisted, however, that the precision and passion that the company put into racecars should be put into building road cars. Since 1948, Ferrari road cars have embodied those legendary standards. A view of Ferrari road cars since 1948 shows the company's high standards of style and their racecar **heritage**.

Ferrari sold the Dino 246 GT between 1968 and 1974.

Power and beauty. The Ferrari GTS Turbo was sold between 1975 and 1985.

Ferrari's "Tailor Made" program allows buyers to personalize every part of their car. Once a buyer makes these choices, they can expect to wait up to two years for delivery.

The F355 Spider went on sale in 1998.

Ferrari's design team works on more than just automobiles. There are Ferrari prancing horse **logos** on clothing, sunglasses, watches, cell phone covers, and even shoes!

The Ferrari F430 Spider was seen on the roads in 2009. Its engine packed 490-horsepower.

The Ferrari 458 Spider hit showrooms in 2011.

FAST FACTS ABOUT FERRARI

Fast Fact 1: The most expensive Ferrari ever sold was a 1957 Testa Rossa. It got about 10 million dollars in a 2011 auction!

Fast Fact 2: The 1962–1964 Ferrari 250 GTO is often called the most sought-after car in the world. Only 39 were built.

Fast Fact 3: In 2002 Ferrari introduced the Enzo Ferrari. Only 400 cars were made. So far 14 of those have been totally destroyed in crashes, at a million dollars each.

A view of Abu Dhabi's Ferrari theme park from the air shows how large it is.

Fast Fact 4: There's a Ferrari theme park in the Mideast nation of Abu Dhabi. Ferrari World Abu Dhabi opened in 2010. It is advertised as "the world's largest indoor theme park."

INTO THE FUTURE

Ferrari held a contest in 2015 to design what the Ferrari of 2040 should look like. The winner was the Manifesto, a design by six students at a **prestigious** design college in France. Besides looking very **futuristic**, Manifesto has amazing "expanding cockpit" doors that open out and up in front!

29

GLOSSARY

endurance (en-DOOR-uhns): the ability to do something difficult for a long time

exotic (ig-ZAH-tik): uncommon, unusual, limited to a few

futuristic (fyoo-chur-is-tik): resembling a time yet to come

heritage (HER-i-tij): an organization's traditions and beliefs

logos (LOH-gohz): distinctive symbols or trademarks that identify a company or organization

prestigious (pres-TIJ-uhs): worthy of great respect and high status

retractable (ri-TRAKT-uh-buhl): able to be drawn back or in

sleek (sleek): smooth and glossy looking

INDEX

SHOW WHAT YOU KNOW

1. Why is the Ferrari 488 called a Spider?
2. How long does it take for the 488 Spider to go from 0 to 60 miles per hour (96.6 kilometers per hour)?
3. In what city is the Ferrari headquarters located?
4. What happened to Enzo Ferrari's factory during World War II?
5. What does the word *formula* mean in Formula One racing?

WEBSITES TO VISIT

www.ferrari.com/en_us

http://auto.ferrari.com/en_EN/ongoing-heritage/company/history

www.revtothelimit.com/ferrari.html

ABOUT THE AUTHOR

Oswald James was born in England, but now lives in the United States. He has always been a racing fan and followed the Ferrari story since childhood. Now he writes and thinks about Ferraris although he has yet to own one. As a teen, his uncle owned a Spider and let him drive it. Since then, he has been into all models of Ferraris.

Meet The Author!
www.meetREMauthors.com

www.rourkeeducationalmedia.com

PHOTO CREDITS: Cover © Art Konovalov; Header art © Petrosg; speedometer art © didis; pages 2-3 © Shaun.P © pages 4-5 © VanderWolf Images; pages 6-7 © lexan; pages 8-9 © Sjoerd van der Wal - istockphoto; pages 10-11 © VanderWolf Images; page 12 © Olga Popova; pages 14-15 © Aiace90; pages 16 © vtornet, 17 © Michael Gulett; page 18 © Lothar Spurzem, page 19 © Morio; page 20 © Luc106, page 20-21 © Writegeist; page 22 © Greg Gjerdingen, page 23 © Marco 56; page 24 © Cloverleaf II, page 25 © Axion23; page 26 © Juan Aunion, page 27 © VanderWolf Images; pages28-29 © Burachet; page 32 author avatar © Yury Shchipakin. Images on pages 2-3, 4-5, 6-7, 10, 12, 26, 27 and 28-29, 32 all from Shutterstock.

Edited by: Keli Sipperley

Cover design by Rhea Magaro
Interior design by: Nicola Stratford   www.nicolastratford.com

Library of Congress PCN Data

Ferrari Spider / Oswald James
 (VROOM! Hot Cars)
 ISBN 978-1-68191-750-4 (hard cover)
 ISBN 978-1-68191-851-8 (soft cover)
 ISBN 978-1-68191-942-3 (e-Book)
Library of Congress Control Number: 2016932713

Rourke Educational Media
Printed in the United States of America, North Mankato, Minnesota

Also Available as: